For Aunt M and Mel
~ CW
For Isabel, with love from Daddy
~ RJ

First published in 2010 by Scholastic Children's Books
Euston House, 24 Eversholt Street
London NW1 1DB
a division of Scholastic Ltd
www.scholastic.co.uk
London ~ New York ~ Toronto ~ Sydney ~ Auckland
Mexico City ~ New Delhi ~ Hong Kong

HB ISBN: 978 1407 10932 9
PB ISBN: 978 1407 10933 6

Printed in Malaysia
1 3 5 7 9 10 8 6 4 2

Papers used by Scholastic Children's Books
are made from wood grown
in sustainable forests.

Crocodiles Need Kisses Too

SCHOLASTIC

Under the moon, on a riverbank, lay a nest full of eggs.
One egg began to **wobble** and **roll**
and **shake**, until . . .

CRACK!

Two beady eyes went **BLINK!** One long snout went **SNAP!**

And lots of sharp, pointy teeth went **SNIP!**

There on the sand was a

snip-o-dile, snap-o-dile,
tiny little crocodile!

The little crocodile looked left.

SNIP!

The little crocodile looked right.

SNAP!

He looked
and looked
and looked . . .

. . . but he was alone on the riverbank.
The little crocodile **snipped** and **snapped** all by himself.

The moon disappeared. The sun came up.
The little crocodile warmed
himself alone on the sand.

But before long he heard

a **cheeping** and a **chirping**.

The little crocodile's heart fluttered – a friend at last!

He peeped over a rock and saw

a mummy sparrow feeding her hungry babies.

The little crocodile was hungry too.

He slithered softly over the sand.

He opened his mouth wide and...

. . . waited his turn to be fed.

"Cheep!
Cheep!" squeaked the baby sparrows in alarm.

"SQUAWK!
SQUAWK!’

screeched their mother.

"It's a snip-o-dile,
snap-o-dile,
very scary crocodile!"
they all shrieked together.

And they flew away
as fast as they could.

The little crocodile
was alone once more.

After a while the little crocodile noticed a **rumbling** in the bushes. A gang of buffalo came down to the river for a drink.

The baby buffalo danced and pranced in the shallow water.

"Here's my chance!" thought the little crocodile.

He **scurried** over the sand towards the baby buffalo and...

. . . leapt into the clear, cool water to join the fun.

"Eek! Eek!" squealed the baby buffalo.

"GRRUMPH! GRRUMPH!"

huffed the big buffalo.

"It's a snip-o-dile,
snap-o-dile,
very scary crocodile!"
they all stamped together.

And they thundered away
as fast as they could.

The little crocodile
was all alone again.

The little crocodile felt sad.

"I would like a mummy to feed me," he sighed.

"I would like to splish and splash in the water with my family," he sniffed.

"I would like a mummy to give me cuddles and kisses!" he cried. A big tear welled up in his beady little eye. It rolled down his long snout.

He opened his mouth wide and was just about to let out a lonely wail...

... when he heard a soft, gentle **purring**.
A mummy tiger was washing her little cub.

She licked his face, and his ears, and even under his chin.
She kissed the little cub all over until he **purred** and **purred**.

"Ooh, that looks nice!" thought the little crocodile.
So he hurried across the sand, crept up
next to the tiger cub and...

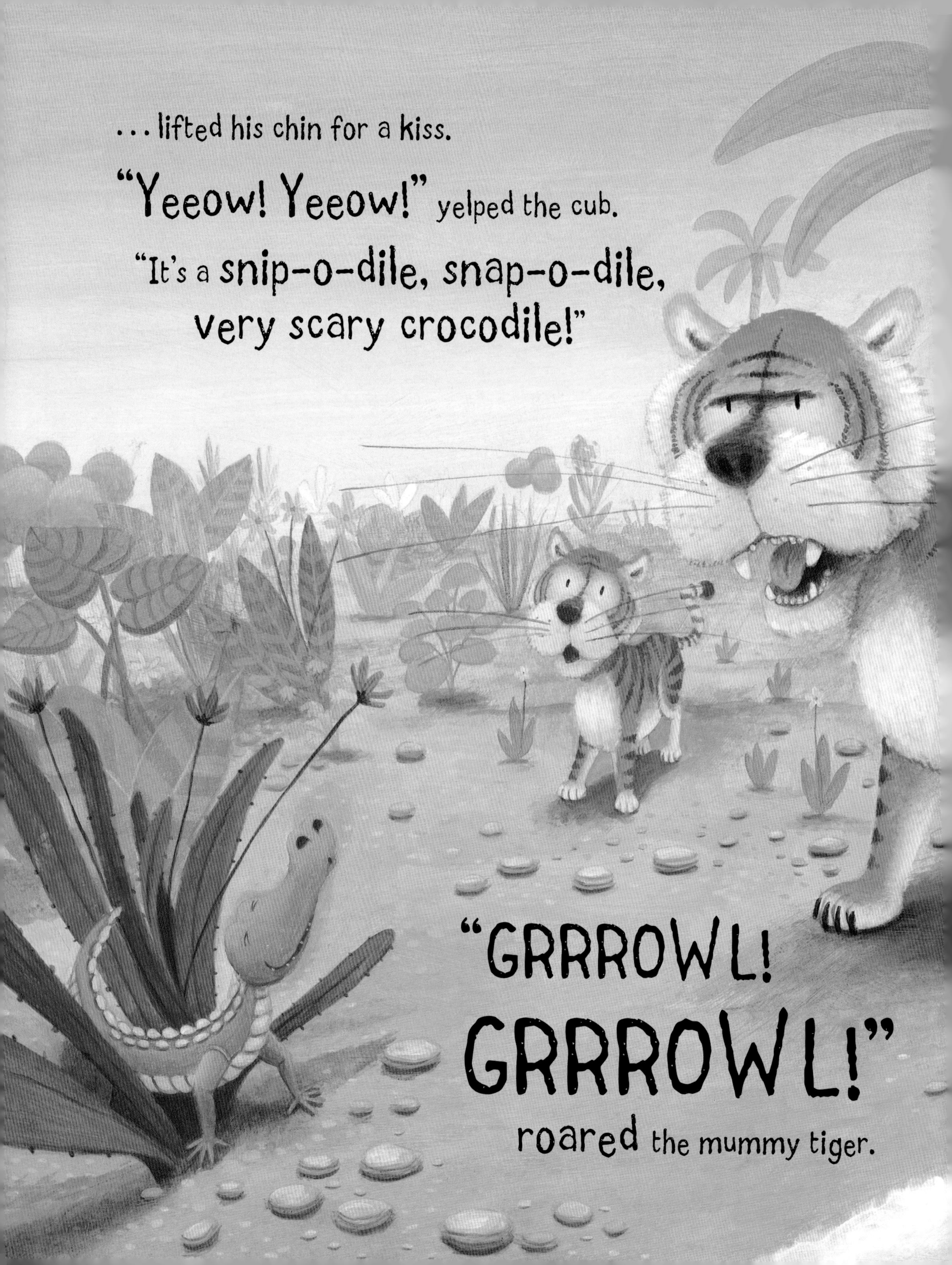

... lifted his chin for a kiss.

"Yeeow! Yeeow!" yelped the cub.

"It's a snip-o-dile, snap-o-dile, very scary crocodile!"

"GRRROWL! GRRROWL!" roared the mummy tiger.

Two fierce eyes.
Lots of big, sharp teeth . . .

"YIKES!"

yelled the terrified
little crocodile, running away
as fast as he could.

He ran and ran until suddenly . . .

Two beady eyes went **BLINK!**

One long snout went **SNAP!**

Lots of sharp, pointy teeth went

SNIP!

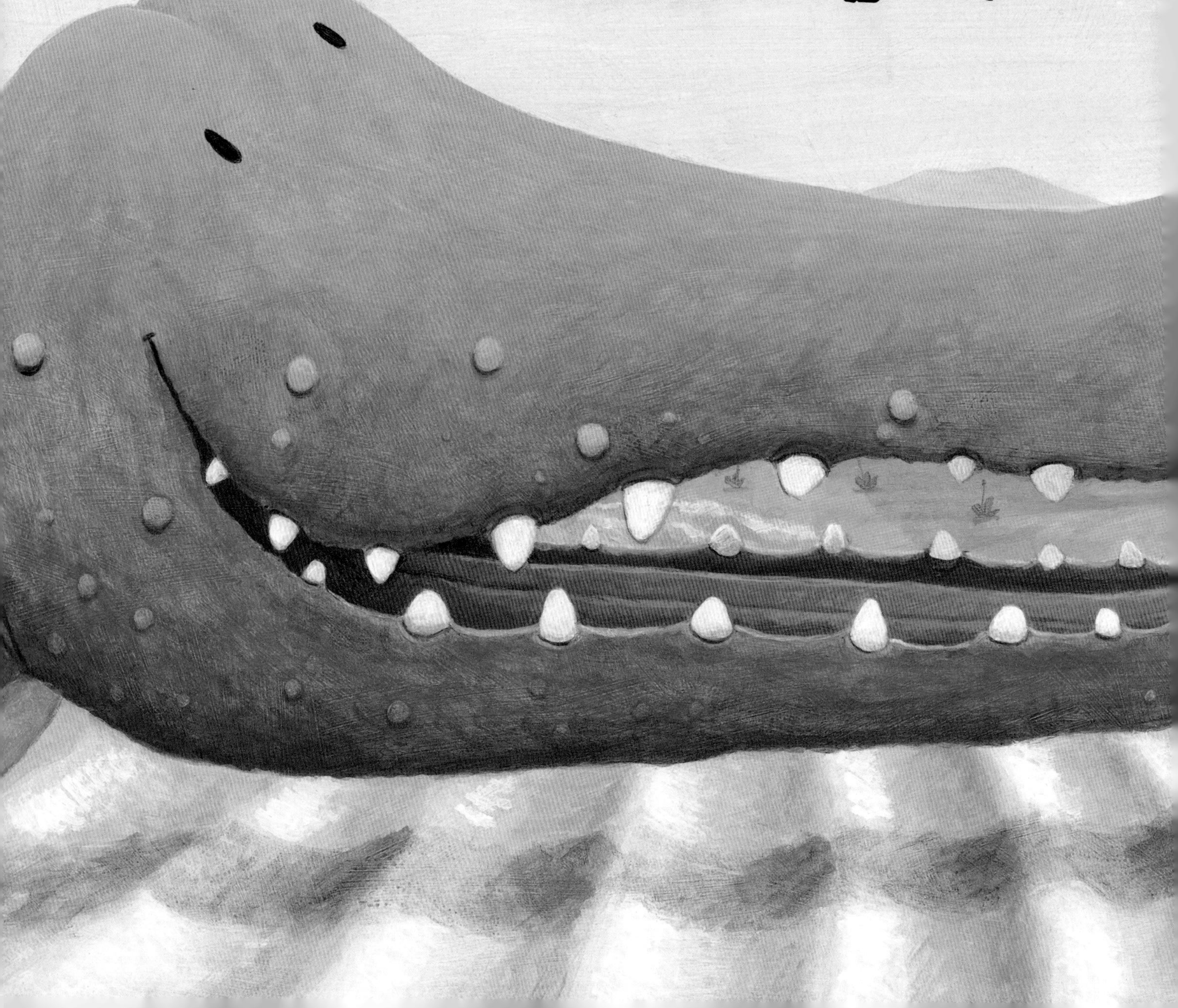

It was a snip-o-dile,
snap-o-dile,
great big crocodile!

The great big crocodile opened
her great wide mouth, crept closer and...

. . . gave her baby a

lovely, snuggly crocodile kiss!

"There, there," she said, "you **are** an early one!"

The little crocodile glowed with happiness
as he **snuggled** close to his mummy.
Together they warmed themselves on the sand.

Very soon, there was a **wobbling**
and a **rolling** and a **shaking**, until finally . . .

CRACK!

Lots of beady eyes went **BLINK!**

Lots of long snouts went **SNAP!**

Hundreds of sharp, pointy teeth went **SNIP!**

The riverbank was full of **snip-o-dile, snap-o-dile, tiny little crocodiles!**

Mummy Crocodile gave each one of her babies a **lovely, snuggly crocodile kiss.**

"After all," she smiled, **"crocodiles need kisses too!"**

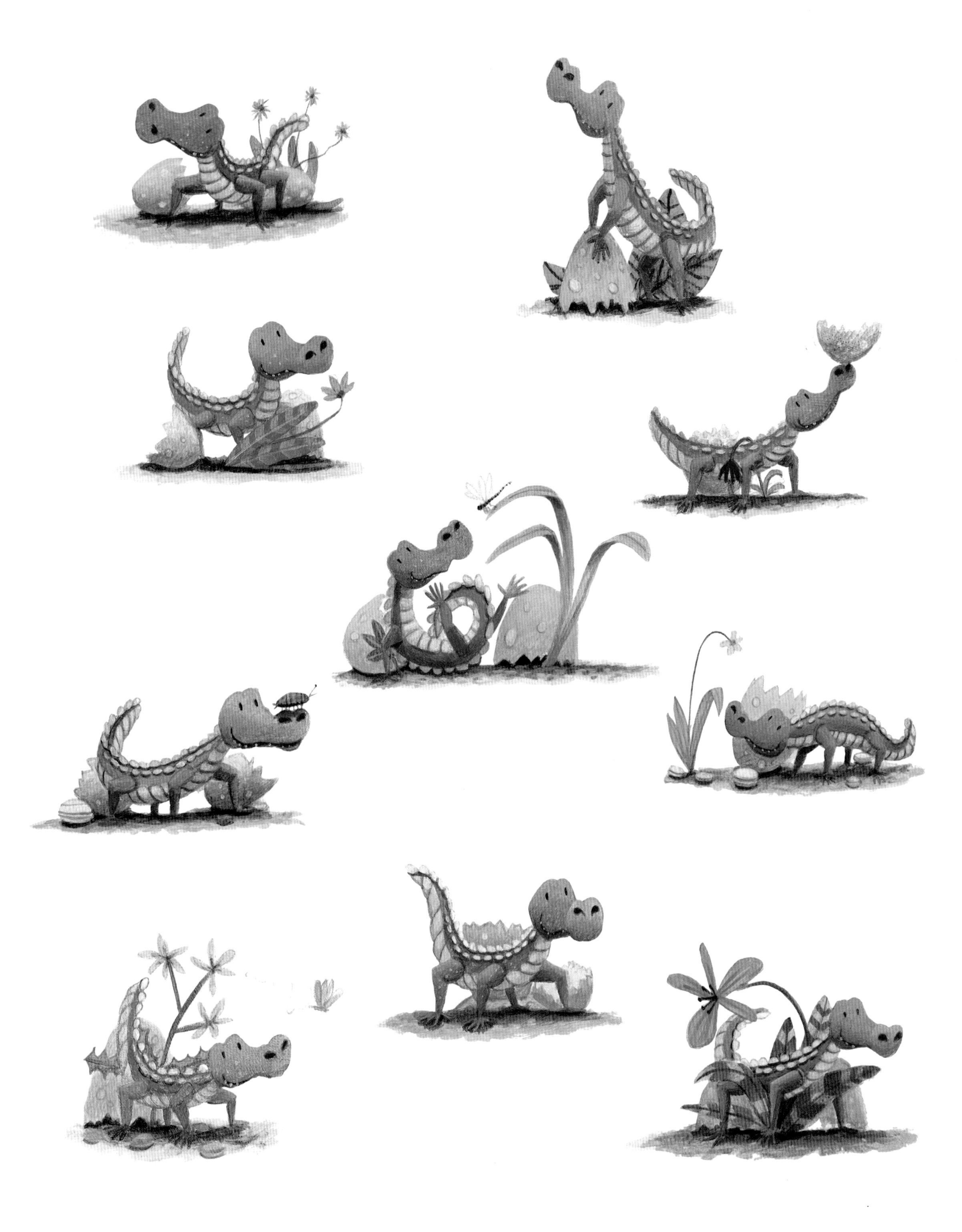

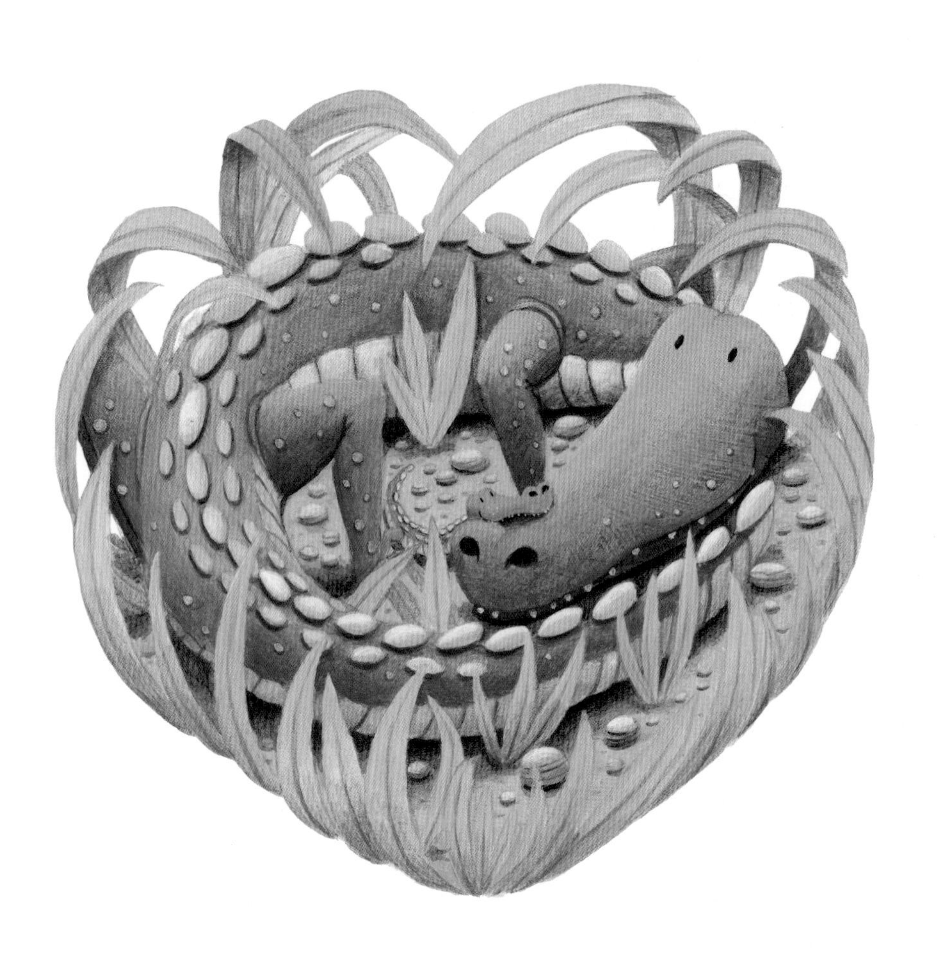